Shoua
and the
Northern Lights Dragon

By Ka Vang

Illustrations by Aimee Hagerty Johnson

About the Reading Together Project:

The Reading Together Project seeks to address the lack of children's books that speak to the experience of being an Asian Pacific Islander (API) child or youth in the United States. The project supports the development of English literacy skills while recognizing cultural heritage, and creating opportunities for children and families to learn about API cultural heritage together.

Book design: Kim Jackson, Dalros Design
Copy editor: Sally Heuer
Proof editor: Eden Bart
Printed by: Grace Wong with Team One Printing

ISBN: 978-0-9884539-0-6

10 9 8 7 6 5 4 3 2 1
First Edition

CONTENTS

DEDICATION

To my parents, Nao Ying Vang and Pang Her Vang,
for showing me the power of magic and being Hmong.
I am realizing that these two things are one and the same.

ACKNOWLEDGMENTS

Special thanks to the Minnesota Humanities Center and their creative staff, including Kham Vang, Casey A. DeMarais, and Junauda Petrus. I would also like to thank the Council on Asian Pacific Minnesotans and their staff, particularly Ilean Her for her leadership.

Thank you to Aimee Johnson for her beautiful illustrations, Sally Heuer for her editing, and Kim Jackson for putting it all together. This book was made possible through your imagination and skills.

Lastly, I would like to thank the following family members for their support: Dr. Mai See Vang Moua, Dr. Aroone Vang, and Brian Charles Tischleder.

CHAPTER 1:

A Fire Ball Dream

~

Crackle! Klump! Snap! As though they spoke, the amber logs illuminating Shoua's campsite spat these words into the night air. The crackles, klumps, and snaps joined the chirping crickets and filled Shoua's ears with happiness. She shut her almond eyes, inhaling the sweet smell of burning birch and recalling how she almost didn't get to go on her first camping trip.

*

"Shoua is not going," her grandfather had announced during family dinner. While her father and brothers were unmoved by his words, Shoua and her mother gasped.

"I turned eleven years old two months ago," Shoua whimpered, twirling her hair with her pointer finger. She twirled her jet-black hair when she was scared, nervous, or anxious. Right now Shoua was all three. Her grandfather ignored her and continued dipping a Hmong sausage in hot pepper sauce before stuffing it into his mouth.

"She can help you collect firewood," pleaded Shoua's mother, passing the plate of Hmong sausage to Shoua after placing a link on her own plate.

"She'll be in the way," countered Shoua's father.

Shoua hated it when grown-ups talked about her as though she were invisible. She also hated it when they made decisions for her and said silly things like "Don't eat the third donut, it's not good for you," followed by "You're too young to understand now, but when you get older you will know why."

Grown-ups underestimated kids. If, she wondered, she held up a neon sign with the words "I AM STILL HERE" on it, would adults stop talking to her as if she wasn't there?

Shoua thought her family underestimated her not because she was a child, but because of something else. No one suspected that underneath her shyness, she was a volcano of courage, brilliance, and magic ready to erupt. What was the disguise that fooled everyone into not seeing her true self? It was nothing more than that she was a girl. One day she would show them all her true self, Shoua thought as her lips curled into a feline smile.

"Just admit it," said Shoua's mother. "You don't want Shoua to go camping because she is a girl."

"No," answered Shoua's father, frantically shaking his head.

"Yes," admitted her grandfather, after taking a sip of water. Shoua looked up at her grandfather as he continued eating his dinner and determining her fate. "Girls should stay home to cook and clean for the men."

"Girls clean, boys camp," scoffed Xeng at Shoua. "Are you a boy?"

Being fifteen years of age and the oldest son in the family, Xeng often repeated things his father and grandfather said, much like a parrot does to imitate its owner. *Except a parrot is smarter*, thought Shoua.

She noticed that there was only one piece of Hmong sausage left, and raised her fork to impale the link when her grandfather swiftly grabbed the plate with the sausage and offered it to her brothers, Xeng and Zong.

"Men eat first, and women eat after the men," her grandfather said, reminding Shoua of the traditional Hmong custom after noticing her disappointment.

"I'm full," said Shoua's ten-year-old brother, Zong, rubbing his bulging belly.

Xeng nodded in agreement.

Her grandfather dumped the link on Shoua's plate with such force that it rolled off Shoua's plate, off the kitchen table, and onto her lap. Shoua stared at the greasy link.

"You can eat the sausage," said Zong. "Five-second rule."

"Yeah, five-second rule," echoed Xeng. "It's not like it fell onto the ground. And even if it did, who cares?"

Shoua stuck her fork in the link and rested it on her plate.

"This will be my first camping and hunting trip since we came to America, and I don't want a girl to ruin it," said her grandfather. After arriving in America eight years ago, he had been too busy working double shifts at the potato factory to do things he enjoyed. Still, he relished coming home covered with grime from sweeping potatoes off the factory floor because it was a physical reminder that he was taking care of his family.

"Hunting in Minnesota will be different than hunting in Laos," he added. "But because we decided to fight with the Americans for freedom against the Communists, there is no way we could stay in Laos after the Communists won the war."

The Vang family had left Laos looking for a better and safer life. If they had stayed, they would have been killed for supporting the Americans. Shoua's mother also reminded her that Hmong girls would have more opportunities in America, but Shoua had seen no evidence of that.

Her mother opened her mouth to say something, but her grandfather cut her off.

"Enough! I'm the head of this family," said Shoua's grandfather. "Shoua is not going."

Shoua turned to him, ready to tell him it was unfair Xeng and Zong got to go camping just because they were boys. But nothing came out. She bit her lips hard, holding back the words.

"Shoua, listen to me," her grandfather said tenderly. "How will you ever be a good wife, daughter, and mother if you are out hunting and fishing? Good Hmong girls don't do these things. I am doing you a big favor by making you stay home."

Tears rained down Shoua's cheeks.

"Your name means 'voice' in Hmong," her mother said as she took a napkin to dry Shoua's cheeks. "Your voice will be heard."

Shoua often spoke in fragmented one-word sentences, "yes" and "no," in Hmong and English. Those simple words mirrored what her family thought about her intelligence. But all the words that she yearned to speak were tightly lodged in her throat, unable to escape. She longed for the day she would clear her throat and the words would erupt like a volcano out of her petite body.

Shoua's mother looked at her father-in-law. "I dreamed last night that one of your grandchildren caught a falling star," she said. "In my dream, that grandchild stood underneath an ebony sky flickering with rainbow colors. A flaming ball of fire fell from the sky into the child's bare hands. This ball was actually a star. It was magical— so magical that trees picked up their roots and walked through the forest in order to see the glowing star in the child's small, soft hands."

Shoua's grandfather was a shaman, a person who heals sick people by connecting with good spirits. As a shaman, he believed that dreams carry special messages.

"Which grandchild?" questioned her grandfather, his eyes darting from Xeng's to Zong's hands.

Shrugging, her mother answered, "I only saw the hands. But I know one of your grandchildren was chosen to do this important task."

Shoua instinctively extended her hands out in front of her, with one hand still holding the fork with the impaled link, hoping her grandfather would notice her hands. Xeng grabbed her forked and bit into the sausage. With a mouthful of food, he muttered, "I'm still hungry."

Shoua knew that when a Hmong person dreams, sometimes that dream has a special meaning. She wondered what her mother's falling star dream meant. Her younger brother was thinking about the dream too.

"I studied stars at school," said Zong. "They can't be caught by people."

"Why not?" asked Shoua.

"Because stars are planets. Because stars are from outer space," replied Zong. "Because they are radioactive. Because—"

"You are making me lose my appetite," said Xeng, swallowing the last of the link.

"Grandfather, what does mother's dream mean?" Shoua asked.

"Dreams don't mean a thing," said Xeng.

"Shoua can help you clean and gut the fish and fowl you catch," pleaded her mother. "These are things Hmong women have always done."

Her grandfather waited a long time before he answered. Finally he looked at his granddaughter and replied, "You can come. You can also gather berries for us while we hunt."

He let out a long sigh before leaving the dinner table and shuffling back to his bedroom.

~

CHAPTER 2:

Five-Toed Tiger

~

A faint line of smoke escaped from the ashen logs, disappearing into the darkness. Overhead, the endless night sky twinkled with stars, some bigger and brighter than others, covering Shoua like an ebony blanket and comforting her. She heard the soft snoring of her father through the tent. He had gone to bed right after it got dark. He was tired from doing most of the work, packing and then setting up the camp. Her father and grandfather slept in one tent while Shoua and her two brothers slept in another. Mr. Grimm, who had sponsored her family eight years ago to come from Laos to America, had also joined them. He slept in his own tent.

A single red flame dancing in the fire pit reminded Shoua of the red signs Mr. and Mrs. Grimm had carried when they had met the

Vangs at the airport. Scribbled on the signs were the words "Proud to be Americans!" and "Born and raised in the USA!" Each family member was given their own miniature America flag to wave as they walked out of the airport in their flip-flops into a blizzard. Trekking across the parking ramp to Mr. Grimm's van, the sleet and wind blew the flag out of Shoua's tiny hand. Her family members dropped their flags after their fingers froze from the cold.

On the way to their south Minneapolis home, Mr. Grimm had reminded the Vangs of how lucky they were.

"My great-grandfather didn't have any help when he came over from Germany," he said with his hawk-like eyes focused on the slippery road.

The Grimms' house was vast, filled with shiny, heavy old things like a grandfather clock and a wooden television set. But the house was missing the laughter of children, Mr. Grimm told Shoua the night they arrived.

"We bought a big house, planning for a big family," Mr. Grimm added. "But Mrs. Grimm and I have to settle for being sponsors."

Mr. Grimm wore a toupee on his head that reminded Shoua of the yellow shaggy rug in the Grimms' living room. Xeng had agreed, adding that the rug and toupee smelled the same. The husband and wife gave the Vangs clothes, took them to the doctors, and found jobs for them. They even bought Shoua her first doll. This gift made Shoua feel guilty for referring to Mr. Grimm as *Mr. Gloom* because he was so negative about their Hmong customs.

Just the faintest sparks lingered in the campfire, so Zong read with the help of a flashlight. To prepare for the trip, he had researched things in northern Minnesota that could hurt or, worse, even kill humans, such as poison ivy, poison oak, and poison mushrooms. And those were just the plants! He also read about snakes, bears, and moose.

"So far I have an inventory of 107 things that can cause death while camping," he told Shoua after catching her staring at him. Zong was the complete opposite of Shoua—she was usually brave, and he was afraid of everything.

"Only 107?" replied Mr. Grimm, coming out of his tent. He sprayed bug repellent on himself and into the air. "It's man against Mother Nature, and Mother Nature always wins. There are more than 107 ways to die out here, believe me, young man."

Mr. Grimm looked like an accountant in the great outdoors. His costume included two pens, one with red ink and one with black ink, and a calculator tucked neatly into the left breast pocket of his shirt. The only indicator that he was camping was an exaggerated safari hat with an abundance of mosquito netting hanging over the sides.

"Keep on reading in English, little brother," said Xeng. "That way the kids at school won't make fun of you because you have a Hmong accent and can't read well, like they do to me."

Without looking up from his book, Zong answered, "Reading is fun."

Mr. Grimm chuckled. "My family stopped reading and speaking German to be real Americans. The only thing I know how to say in German is bier and sauerkraut. The key to being a new American is taking the best of the old culture and infusing it with the new culture."

Zong didn't look up from his book, but nodded to acknowledge Mr. Grimm. Shoua wondered if Mr. Grimm was aware that his words contradicted all the things he'd done to help her family become "real" Americans. If becoming an adult meant contradicting herself all the time like Mr. Grimm did, then she didn't want to grow up.

Shoua's grandfather emerged from his tent.

"For once my shaman spirits and the American doctors agree on something," he said. "Getting fresh air is good for my health."

"Ever since your family came to America, I've been planning the perfect camping trip for all of you," replied Mr. Grimm. "But Grandfather Vang was too busy working at the potato factory to camp. And none of you wanted to come without him."

"Getting away from the potato factory is good for my weak heart," her grandfather agreed. "The last time my heart was this weak, I stared into the eyes of a demon-tiger."

Her grandfather sat down in front of the fire and stoked it with a long stick, causing the flames to flare. He cleared his throat as if he was going to make a grand announcement.

"When I was a little boy, I killed a demon-tiger who was stalking my parents' farm. My shaman spirits helped me slay the creature."

Mr. Grimm rolled his eyes, but Shoua was the only one who noticed. Mr. Grimm didn't like it when Shoua's grandfather talked about being a shaman. He thought the spirits and magic her grandfather experienced weren't real.

"The tiger's eyes were as black as onyx, eyes of a demon," her grandfather said as if he was in a trance. "It had been a hot spring. The air was so thick and humid you could cut it with a knife. The winds hissed as though they were trying to give us a message. The tiger appeared out of nowhere and disappeared just as quickly,

leaving behind death.
For weeks, it killed
and ate our chickens
and pigs at night.
We knew it was a
demon-tiger by the
bloody paw-prints it
left behind; both its front and back paws had
five toes."

Shoua's grandfather leaned over the fire and
opened his eyes; his face was bathed in the yellow
glow, with dancing flames reflected in his eyes.
Zong and Shoua also leaned in, pulled by the
power of his story.

"The demon-tiger never came out during the
day, only at night when we were asleep. Finally,
my frustrated father gathered the remaining
livestock and took them to our uncle's farm. The
next day while the women plowed the land, the

men went to hunt for the tiger. I pleaded to go with the men, but was told I was too young. My father even said I could ruin the hunt with my youth. I was left at the house to do chores. So I devised a plan to follow the men and slay the tiger myself. I would prove to my father that I was a man."

The fire flared as Shoua's grandfather continued his story. "I waited until the men left. Then I put on my hat and slung my bow and arrow on my back, ready to sprint out of the hut when— *tap...tap...tap*. There was a knock at the door. I asked who it was, and a smooth voice answered that it was a traveler seeking shelter after a long journey. I opened the door. In front of me was the tiger, eyes black as onyx, eyes of a demon. It was three times larger than a normal tiger, with radiant orange and black fur. The tiger's eyes peered right into my soul like it wanted to eat it for lunch. The creature grinned and deliberately licked its lips with its tongue as though it read my thoughts. I attempted to run away from the beast, but I stumbled to the ground. I was too scared to move. The tiger slowly and deliberately circled me. I was so terrified I couldn't look at its face, so I looked down. That's when I saw his bloody five-toed paws."

Chills ran through Shoua's body as she imagined her grandfather as a boy, helpless at the feet of the huge beast. She twirled her hair, wondering if she would be as brave as him if she ever found herself at the feet of a large beast.

"There was nothing left for me to do but pray to the ancestors for help. I was a good kid who helped my parents, clan, and village. I prayed for the spirits of the jungle, mountains, valleys, rivers, and sky to stop the tiger from hurting me. The heavens heard my call, guiding my hands to the bow and arrow, and I aimed it at the beast's heart. The arrow roared like thunder through our hut, moving like a bolt of lightning as it impaled the tiger. The cat's body lit up in an electric flash," said Shoua's grandfather, leaning even closer to his grandchildren, staring them in the eyes, with fists clenched tight.

"The demon-tiger lay with his eyes closed peacefully. I was saved by my ancestors and the good spirits of the land," he said.

Shoua and Zong were speechless as they listened to their grandfather tell his story.

Xeng was the first to say anything. "That is a stupid story. Come on, tigers don't speak. Thunder and lightning don't appear out of nowhere."

Xeng hated everything, Shoua thought. Her father and grandfather expected a lot from Xeng because he was the oldest son, and Xeng reacted by being negative about everything.

"We also have a story like that. It's called *Little Red Riding Hood*," said Mr. Grimm. "Not sure which monster is scarier, a wolf or a tiger. Tell the folktale again with a wolf."

Shoua's grandfather lowered his head to the ground, embarrassed by Mr. Grimm's and Xeng's comments. Shoua wanted to shield her grandfather from the remarks, but nothing came out of her mouth. Instead she felt as though she had swallowed those words and they were now lodged in her throat.

Her grandfather cleared his throat again, stating, "It's getting late. We better get to sleep."

~

CHAPTER 3:

Northern Lights Surprise

~

The sound of leaves rustling in the wind pulled Shoua out of her sleeping bag, out of the tent, and into the blazingly colorful night sky. Her mouth opened to a big O as she tilted her head to stare at the heavens. Streaks of red and blue lines danced across the sky. The dancing lights reminded Shoua of neon cotton candy moving across a black blanket. Even the crickets seemed to stop chirping to watch the lights. Shoua was the first to come out of the tent; the men trickled out of their tents moments later.

"It's dragons!" exclaimed Shoua's grandfather, hopping excitedly and pointing at the lights. "When we see lights moving across the heavens like this, it means dragons have come out of hiding and are about to come to earth."

Her grandfather often told folktales about

dragons, explaining how the magical creatures traveled between the human world and spirit world.

"The lights are called the *aurora borealis*, or northern lights," offered Mr. Grimm. "Caused by energetically charged particles colliding with atoms in the high-altitude atmosphere."

Zong agreed with him, adding, "I read that in a book."

"There are no dragons in those lights," barked Xeng.

Shoua watched her grandfather's face turn from pure bliss to disappointment. His mouth opened to say something, then closed tightly.

"Grandfather, I don't see dragons in the dancing lights, but I know they are in there," she squeaked like a mouse at his feet.

Shoua's words were a balm on his hurt ego. Mr. Grimm's and Xeng's constant criticism about everything Hmong eroded her grandfather's spirit. But as his glum face glanced down at her, she felt he would have preferred Zong defending him instead of his granddaughter.

The peaceful night sky changed with the sound of thunder. Bolts of lightning splattered through the dancing lights. The winds changed and howled like a hungry wolf, threatening to blow their tents over. The red and blue lights swirled into a colossal cloud before opening up like a curtain. Suddenly a flaming ball raced like a comet through the curtain of lights toward earth. Shoua instinctively clutched her grandfather's trembling hands. The ball of flames raced toward them. Mr. Grimm shook his head in disbelief and gasped, "Oh man, I didn't plan for this!"

Xeng, Zong, and their father held on to each other. The flaming ball looked like it was going to slam into their campsite, but at the last moment, it moved higher into the sky and passed over them, leaving behind a trail of smoke and disappearing into the black forest. There were no cricket chirps, no crackle from the fire—only the sounds of their heaving breaths. For several long minutes, no one spoke. Then Zong broke the silence.

"Number 108, death by flaming ball from the sky," he uttered.

Shoua turned to her grandfather and hollered, "Grandfather! Mr. Grimm! Let's go and find the ball that fell from the sky!"

Shoua hopped up and down like a bunny, pulling her grandfather's arm in the direction of the fallen fire ball. The old man had an expression on his face that she had never seen before. Could it be apprehension, or even fear?

"It's not safe, Shoua," replied Mr. Grimm. "It's not safe."

"Mr. Grimm is right. You should go to sleep," said her grandfather. "We should all sleep."

"We have to drive into Ely tomorrow and report this to the police," Mr. Grimm added. Ely was a nearby town. "We'll tell them a comet fell from the sky."

"Something fell from the sky, not a comet, but a—"

Shoua couldn't hear the last of her grandfather's words because he had crawled into his tent. Frowning, Shoua walked slowly back to the tent she shared with her brothers.

*

Shoua's eyes closed peacefully and her chest heaved in a rhythm suggesting she was asleep. Yet under her sleeping bag, her pointer finger diligently twirled chunks of her hair. Shoua did this over and over again as she contemplated whether she would go and look for the fallen fire ball. She heard her mother's words echo in her ears, telling everyone that a child in their family had caught a fallen star, and Shoua knew she was the chosen one. Years of being told she wasn't smart filled Shoua with doubt and fear as she lay in her sleeping bag. Then, as if they had their own will, her legs kicked off the sleeping bag, and she crept out of the tent like a shadow.

~

CHAPTER 4:

Shoua and Zong Go on an Adventure

~

The sun peeked over the eastern horizon along a row of pine trees. It reminded Shoua of melted butter poured over the treetops. She scanned the fire pit filled with ashes and charred logs from the night before. A faint yellow hue covered the land, though it was not quite morning and the night still lingered. Shoua silently tiptoed into the tent she shared with Zong and Xeng. Gently pushing them awake, she pressed her pointer finger to her lips, signaling them to be silent.

"Shoua, why did you wake us up?" whispered Xeng, rubbing his eyes.

"Shhhhhh," she replied.

"I was in the middle of an awesome dream where I was eating an endless bowl of pho noodle soup," said Zong, wiping the drool from his lips.

"Help me find the fire ball," asked Shoua.

Zong looked puzzled.

"Why do you need to find the fire ball?" asked Xeng. "I thought it wasn't safe."

"Something is pulling me to find the fallen fire ball," she answered.

"If there is a fallen star, and that is a big *if*," said Xeng, "only a boy would have the smarts to find it."

Shoua hated it when Xeng sounded like their grandfather. She hated when Xeng sounded like Mr. Grimm too. For once in her life, she wanted him to stop being a parrot and come up with an original thought.

"Don't wake me up again," said Xeng, zipping up his sleeping bag. "Don't even think about going, you won't find it anyway."

"Good night, Shoua," said Zong before he closed his eyes.

She heard their steady snores within minutes. Shoua couldn't go back to sleep. She felt a magnetic pull from the direction of the fire ball. While playing with her hair, she concocted another plan. But this plan involved only one brother.

"Zong," Shoua whispered while poking him. "Please help me."

Shoua wanted—no, she *needed*—Zong's help. She needed his mind. He read books about starting fires, surviving encounters with bears, evading moose, identifying deadly mushrooms, and recovering from poison ivy.

"No," he muttered with his eyes still closed. "There are dozens of ways to die in northern Minnesota. I am certainly not going to go explore number 108, death by fire ball falling from the sky."

"If you go with me, I'll make your favorite dish—pho noodle soup—for a whole week."

Zong knew that Shoua could make his dream a reality.

"We can't go without packing my flashlight and book on northern Minnesota wildlife," he said. "You have to pack them. You have to lead the way. I'm not totally awake yet."

As Shoua packed, she tried to hide the smile radiating from her face.

*

Shoua's feet galloped down a marked trail, with Zong trying to keep up. The rustling leaves of the birch trees whispered secret directions to Shoua. The sway of northern pines from the breeze showed her where to turn when she came to forks in the trail. She saw an oak branch move to point her in the right direction. Zong didn't notice the signs because they were not meant for him. Instead, the chilly morning air, thirst, and hunger eroded his senses, causing him to be frustrated.

"We should turn around," Zong begged, gasping for breath.

"We are almost there," Shoua assured him.

"How do you know?"

"The same way grandfather knows about healing people. The same way grandfather sees things that we can't see," she answered. "I just know."

Two deer, a doe and a buck, leaped from the bushes and dashed in the direction that Shoua and Zong had just come from. Moments later, half a dozen rabbits scurried past them; some even darted right near their feet, headed in the same direction as the deer. The chilly morning air was gone, replaced by the midday heat.

All of a sudden a black bear emerged from the

bushes. Its watery eyes looked alarmed as it stared into Shoua's brown eyes. For a moment Shoua and the black bear seemed connected by a singular thought, but the spell was broken by Zong.

"Shoua, don't run," he said cautiously. "Number 6 on my list, death by black bear—not to be confused with number 7, death by brown bear."

"Shhh....," replied Shoua.

The bear tilted its head and growled before lunging toward them.

Zong held his breath and closed his eyes, firmly expecting to be slashed by claws. Shoua's eyes locked with the bear's. It halted in front of her and opened its mouth so wide she could see its sharp fangs and blue tongue. Shoua's face was bathed in the bear's hot breath. Then, it licked her entire face, swirling its tongue and leaving trails of blue saliva on her cheeks before it abruptly dashed away on all fours.

Zong let out a thunderous roar of laughter while patting his chest, stomach, and thighs to make sure all his body parts were still there.

"We have to turn around!" he blurted.

Shoua's determined almond eyes answered him.

"We just escaped death! Besides, deer, rabbits, and even a bear are running from something," he said. "So should we."

He noticed Shoua's dazed expression and went right up to her, screaming, "Shoua, are you *listening* to me?"

Shoua spoke in a trance-like voice. "The bear talked to me, and I understood it."

"Now you sound like grandfather."

"The bear said that something strange, even magical fell—"

"Stop! There is nothing in any of the books I have read that even *remotely* suggests bears can talk to kids!" Zong hollered. "Shoua, I'm tired and hungry. Let's go back."

"Exactly, the bear knew you were hungry and said blueberries are ready to be picked along a stream nearby."

"Bears don't give out advice on eating," said Zong.

"Its tongue was blue from all the berries it feasted on, and it licked me so I would know how delicious the blueberries were—"

Shoua's words were interrupted by loud moans from an animal. The moans sounded like a trombone calling for help. They caused Shoua's heart to flutter as fast as hummingbird wings. An electric surge of triumph coursed through her body: she knew she was close to finding the fire ball.

"That noise does not sound good," said Zong, who pivoted and started walking away. Shoua sprinted toward him, grabbing him by the shoulder.

"Zong, I can't do this without you. I need your help," she said with tears cascading down her cheeks. "I'm so close."

"Why is it so important to find the fire ball?"

The words were locked securely in her throat. Shoua coughed, clearing her throat, and struggled to let the words out.

"B-B-Be-Being born a girl, I feel like a bird with its wings clipped," she said. "Finding the fire ball will give me the wings to fly."

Shoua unconsciously massaged her strained throat with both her hands.

"Alright, I'll continue," said Zong. "You lead."

Shoua twirled her hair as she sprinted toward the trombone moans, her heart filled with victory and her head filled with images of her grandfather complimenting her for finding the fire ball. Zong couldn't keep up because his heavy backpack was filled with food, a flashlight, and his wildlife book. His heart and head were filled with fear. They jogged until they came to a clearing among a grove of northern pines. The flaming ball had charred the pines and rocks in its path. In the middle of the clearing was a giant hole the size of a truck. Shoua raced toward the hole.

"Wait, Shoua!" Zong cried. "You don't know what's inside!"

Shoua didn't hear his words. The mystery inside the hole pulled her legs forward. She stopped at the edge and began to twirl her hair. Zong was completely out of breath when he reached her.

Shoua gasped in amazement as she peered into the black hole. A smile extended across her face, practically touching her ears. With shimmery gold scales on its belly and emerald scales covering the rest of its body, a dragon was curled in the center of the hole. The creature resembled a colossal eel with two strong arms and legs. The dragon lay on its side with its quivering arms covering its belly. Its eyes glowed like amber as it blinked its long brown lashes. Shoua saw her reflection and something else—fear—in the dragon's eyes.

She locked eyes with the dragon and tried to communicate with it telepathically like she did with the bear.

"I can't believe Grandfather was right!" Zong yelled. Shoua had forgotten about her younger brother during the excitement of finding the dragon.

"The fire ball that fell last night wasn't a star," said Shoua. "It was a dragon, curled into a ball."

"*That* was not in my book on northern Minnesota wildlife!"

Zong's loud voice frightened the dragon, who

quivered in response. Shoua cupped her brother's chin in her hands, pulling his face to hers and gazing deeply into his eyes. Zong was silenced by her stare. After motioning for him to stay put, she slid down the hole to the dragon. Zong frantically grasped at her, not wanting her to go into the hole, but his hands only captured air. Shoua landed elegantly on the charred earth with the grace of a dancer.

She extended her hand to the dragon, who sniffed it. Confident the creature was comfortable with her, she leaned closer, looking directly into its eyes. She kneeled and gently stroked its scaly nostrils. The dragon's nose was as cold as a glacier, and smooth as silk.

She looked even deeper into the dragon's eyes and connected with it. She then moved her hands to stroke the creature's icy cheeks. Fear evaporated from its forlorn eyes, replaced with hope.

It slowly moved its hands away from where it had covered its belly. Shoua saw a large gash in its stomach. Golden blood trickled from the cut.

"Help," the dragon whispered.

~

CHAPTER 5:

Help Heal a Dragon

~

The dragon's call for help was carried by the morning breeze, across the northern pine treetops, over a rushing stream, and through the meadows straight into Shoua's grandfather's tent. The plea pinched the old man awake.

"A dragon!" he yelled, leaping from his sleeping bag. The old man dashed out of his tent.

"Zong! Zong!" he muttered, poking his head into the children's tent, only to find Xeng sprawled asleep on the ground.

"Where is Zong?" Grandfather repeatedly asked, scurrying around the campsite like a chicken with its head cut off.

Mr. Grimm and Shoua's father emerged from their tents, alarmed by the old man's thundering words.

"Mr. Vang?" a puzzled Mr. Grimm asked. "Mr. Vang, are you okay?"

"Father, please calm down," pleaded Shoua's father as he grabbed the older man in order to get him to stop moving erratically. "Think about your weak heart."

"My grandchild has found a dragon," replied Shoua's grandfather. "My shaman spirits told me my grandchild has found a dragon."

"Shoua and Zong are gone!" exclaimed Shoua's father after peeking into the children's tent and only seeing Xeng. "We have to find them."

"When Zong returns with a dragon," her grandfather said jovially, "Shoua will come back with him."

"Why would Zong go chasing after a dragon?" Shoua's father asked quizzically. "Xeng, get out here!"

Xeng emerged from his tent and gingerly

stretched like a cat, half asleep.

"Where are your brother and sister?" demanded his father.

"Zong woke me up this morning to go and find the fire ball. Shoua went with him," he lied to the men. Xeng justified the lie by telling himself it was just a half lie; besides, it was the lie his grandfather wanted to hear. Xeng agreed with people and repeated things they said to make them happy—not because he wanted to please them, but because he wanted them off his back.

"You let your little brother and sister go into the forest alone! Why would you do that? What if they come across a wild animal or fall off a cliff? I cannot believe this!" Now his father was hollering. "You are the oldest child, oldest son, your role is to protect Shoua and Zong! You failed your duty—"

"Stop yelling," Mr. Grimm interrupted. "It's

not going to do any good. Let's go find them before they get hurt."

"There is no need to worry," said Shoua's grandfather. "Zong and Shoua are safe. They are with a powerful dragon."

"Mr. Vang!" Now it was Mr. Grimm's voice that rose three octaves. "I planned the perfect camping trip. Your grandchildren ruined it by running away! I'm your sponsor. Mrs. Grimm would never forgive me if we came back from our trip without Zong and Shoua. I would never forgive myself."

"Zong has been chosen do an important task," Shoua's grandfather answered serenely. "He is the one chosen to find a dragon."

"Father, you wait at the campsite just in case the children come back," Shoua's father said. "Xeng will come with me. Mr. Grimm, you can head in the opposite direction."

Shoua's grandfather watched as the three disappeared into the woods determined to find the children.

Her father and Xeng returned to the campsite around noon, without Shoua and Zong. They appeared defeated. Minutes later, Mr. Grimm emerged from the woods looking like he had spent days lost in the wilderness. Sweat stains soaked the underarms of his white cotton button-up shirt. The two pens placed neatly in his right shirt pocket that morning were now noticeably broken and crooked. What's worse, the red pen bled, making it look like Mr. Grimm had been shot in the chest and had blood spurting toward his belly.

"Maybe I should drive into Ely for help," Mr. Grimm said as he walked past a plate of food with hamburger and rice that Shoua's grandfather extended to him. "I'm not going to fail this family as your sponsor. I made a promise to take care of you when you came to this country."

*

Shoua and the dragon spoke to each other without moving their mouths, without even a gesture. The language that flowed between them could not be heard by Zong or anyone else. It turned out the dragon was a girl, just like Shoua—even the same age. Her name was Nanee, which means "little snake" in Hmong. She came from a dimension that existed between earth and heaven. Unicorns, fairies, and sea monsters roamed Nanee's universe. Magic flowed through the veins of all the creatures in her world like blood flowed through all the creatures in Shoua's world.

"I came to your world last night to find an iridescent green feather from a loon's head. The feathers are special; they can heal dragons."

Shoua sensed Nanee becoming weaker with each passing moment.

"My grandfather is sick, so my parents wanted to travel to the human world to get loon feathers," Nanee continued. "We needed one feather to touch my grandfather to heal him. My parents didn't want to come during the night because there would be no light to guide them. I wanted to prove to my family that a girl dragon can accomplish a great task, like find a healing loon feather."

"I understand," replied Shoua. "I came to find you to prove to my grandfather that I was just as smart as my brothers."

"I entered your world through a portal without my parents' permission, without them knowing," Nanee continued. "They were right, it was too dark to see, and I ended up lost. Then something strange happened: I was hit by lightning and plunged to earth."

Magic in the form of liquid ooze spilled from the cut on Nanee's belly.

"Without magic, I can't return home."

Shoua continued to stroke Nanee's scaly cheeks.

"I can help you get two loon feathers," Shoua told Nanee. "One feather to heal you, and a second feather to heal your grandfather."

Shoua's and Nanee's words, like their lives, intertwined and locked together for a common goal. They both needed each other to prove to their skeptical family members that girls could be heroes.

"I can't fly to my portal unless I am healed," the dragon said. "Once I am healed, I can go home. We dragons have the magical power to make ourselves invisible to humans, so they can't touch, see, smell, or hear us. I have just enough power to make myself invisible one more time. I can communicate with you because you have magic inside of you," said Nanee. "We have to be careful who we show ourselves to, because there are people who hate dragons or, even worse, would harm them. Dragons rarely show themselves to humans because in the past, humans hunted us down and killed us almost to extinction. In order to save our kind, we have to permanently live in the magic world. I am breaking the dragon law of making contact with humans, but I need—"

Nanee let out a long and painful trombone moan, unable to finish her sentence.

"I won't let you down," Shoua replied telepathically to Nanee.

~

CHAPTER 6:

Zong Goes Loon-y for a Feather

~

Everything Zong knew about loons he learned from reading books. Besides knowing the loon was the Minnesota state bird, he also learned where loons live, how they swim, and what they eat.

"Yeah, but do you know how to get *feathers* from a loon?" questioned Shoua. She had told her brother about the dragon's plight and why they needed to find the feathers. Together they followed a babbling brook, hoping it would lead them to a lake and, eventually, to loons.

Insulted, Zong stopped and replied, "I believed in you, now it is your turn to believe in me."

Zong put his lips together like he was about to whistle, then covered his mouth with his hands and yodeled. The eerie wails coming from Zong echoed through the quiet forest.

"Big sister, that is a loon call," he bragged. "That is how we will catch a loon and get its feathers."

They walked for what seemed like hours as Zong periodically stopped to munch wild blueberries growing near the banks of the brook.

"Come *on*," pleaded Shoua.

"I haven't eaten all day," countered Zong.

"Nanee needs me!"

"Shoua, chill out," he said, stuffing handfuls of berries in his mouth, blue juices running down his chin. "Hey, the bear was right. These blueberries are delicious."

"I heard blueberries can also kill you," Shoua lied.

"Well, too much of anything can kill you," Zong replied. "Even a loon feather can kill you."

"How?"

"You can be tickled to death."

When he wasn't eating, Zong pointed out

poisonous mushrooms and other things on his list that could kill them.

They followed the brook until it emptied into a crystal-clear lake. Shoua saw multicolored rocks at the bottom of the shallow waters near the shore. The rocks reminded her of Nanee's scales. A dark, gray mist shrouded the lake, making the day seem more like night. In the distance they heard the call of loons. Shoua and Zong grinned and high-fived.

Again, Zong covered his mouth with his hands. His fingers fluttered like butterfly wings as the eerie sound of a loon call emanated from Zong's mouth. After a few minutes, three large black and white birds with beady red eyes emerged from the fog and swam toward them.

"This is too easy," Shoua said.

As though they had heard her words, the three loons flexed their wings, exposing their huge wingspans, and disappeared under the water.

Zong called several more times, but the loons stayed away.

Shoua panted and began to twirl her hair ferociously with both of her pointer fingers, huffing, "Why, *why* did I open my big mouth? I jinxed us! What are we going to do? I'll never get grandfather's approval if I don't get the loon feathers and help Nanee."

"Why is it so important to have grandfather's approval?" Zong asked.

Shoua thought for a long time before answering. "I'm tired of eating your and Xeng's leftovers."

"I understand. But do this for yourself. If you don't like yourself, you will forever be chasing the approval of others."

Shoua thought that sometimes Zong was much more mature and brainy than the average ten-year-old.

"How did you become so wise?" she asked.

"Books. Everything I know I learned from books. Speaking of books..."

Zong pulled his enormous book about northern Minnesota wildlife from his backpack. He opened the book and scanned the table of contents before finding the page he needed. In a matter of seconds, Zong quickly read those pages, muttering sentences under his breath. Shoua heard Zong utter the word "loon" multiple times. He closed his book with a loud *thud!* and pulled a flashlight from his backpack.

"We will get our loon feather with this," Zong said, proudly pointing to the flashlight. "Promise to be quiet."

Holding his flashlight, Zong slid into the lake's foggy expanse, which was filled with bulrushes and cattails, hiding him from his sister. Soon Shoua heard the eerie call of a loon coming from her brother in the marsh. Suddenly to her surprise, a loon lured by Zong's call swam out of the mist and disappeared into the cattails. She saw Zong leap in after it and emerge from the thick cattails with the loon in one arm and the flashlight in another arm. The loon was unable to move, mesmerized by the flashlight shining in its eyes.

"Shoua!" he called. "Come quick and pluck two feathers from its head!"

As she waded as quickly as possible toward her younger brother, she could almost taste the triumph of being a hero to Nanee, to her grandfather—and to herself.

*

Later, as Shoua and Zong walked back to the dragon with two loon feathers tucked safely into Shoua's pants pocket, she asked her younger brother how he knew of the trick with the flashlight.

"I told you, everything I learned I read in books," he said confidently. "Researchers tag loons by using a light to daze them, so I just did the same with my flashlight."

Sparks of pride flared up inside Shoua as she imagined the look on her grandfather's face when she announced she saved a dragon. It was a feeling she was not used to having. Her grandfather would have no choice but to see her as an equal to her brothers.

As they walked through a grove of northern pine saplings and turned the bend in the trail, the children saw a forest ranger walking toward them. Shoua became anxious. Was the ranger after her and Zong for plucking the feather from a loon? Maybe the ranger had found the dragon? Endless scenarios raced through Shoua's mind as she unconsciously raised her right pointer finger to twirl her hair. Her dream of proving herself to her grandfather began to vanish as the ranger got closer.

"What are you kids doing out here?" the ranger asked. "Where are your parents?"

"We are camping nearby with our family," answered Shoua confidently. She scanned the ranger's face, looking for clues to see if he believed her, but his face was too hairy for her to see anything. All she saw was a shaggy beard and red nose under the ranger hat.

"I'm Ranger Ron," he said. "Something fell from the sky last night—at least we've gotten several reports from campers that something fell. But I'm not sure what it is. I just came from over there"— he pointed in back of him —"and there is a hole in the ground the size of a truck. But no meteor. Nothing."

Shoua smelled shaving lotion and stale tobacco on Ranger Ron. The shaving lotion didn't make sense: he had so much hair and whiskers he looked like Smokey the Bear. Except he wasn't as cute as Smokey, and Smokey would never be caught chewing or smoking tobacco.

"I'm calling this in to my superiors to see what they want me to do," he added. "But I don't want the two of you going over there. The area around the crater is charred. It might be contaminated, or worse."

Shoua and Zong nodded, but with her left hand, Shoua crossed her fingers in her jeans pocket, and with her right hand, she patted the feathers.

The children walked with the ranger until they came to a fork in the road.

"Kids, my truck is in this direction," he said, pointing to the path on the right.

"Darn, our campsite is in that direction," Shoua said, pointing to the left path.

"Be careful," Ranger Ron said. "I'll check on you guys later after I call my superiors for an update."

They waited until they were sure Ranger Ron was gone before turning around. *Nanee must have made herself invisible to Ranger Ron*, Shoua thought. She was worried about the dragon. Shoua knew she and her brother needed to get back to the hole immediately. Then her ears perked up as she heard Nanee calling her name.

"Did you hear that?" she asked Zong.

"Hear what?" he answered.

Of course Zong couldn't hear Nanee, Shoua thought; he didn't share the same connection with the dragon that she did. Again, she heard Nanee's moaning: "Hurry, hurry, hurry..."

"Nanee needs me *now*!" yelped Shoua before sprinting down the path toward the dragon.

Zong stumbled to keep up with her. Shoua ran through the thick grove of northern pine saplings they had passed earlier. But this time the branches clung to her, imprisoning her. As she struggled to break free from their grip, the tree branches scratched her skin and tore at her clothes. With a loud "AWWW!" Shoua mustered all her strength and broke free, only to slam right into something that caused her to tumble to the ground. She tilted her head to look up and saw Mr. Grimm, his dark face framed by a halo of sunlight. Shoua closed her eyes and took a deep breath before getting up to face Mr. Grimm.

~

CHAPTER 7:

Nanee Is Not Alone

~

"There you are!" Mr. Grimm said. "We have been worried sick about you and Zong. Where is he?"

Zong emerged from the grove of trees, panting with exhaustion.

"The two of you are in big trouble!" hollered Mr. Grimm, his words echoing through the woods.

"No!" cried Shoua, twirling her hair in frustration. "I have to save the dragon!"

Mr. Grimm laughed at her words.

Shoua tried to walk pass Mr. Grimm, but he grabbed her arms.

"*There is no dragon*," he said firmly.

With a burst of strength, she yanked free from his grip and darted off. Her hair flew in the wind like fierce ebony whips. Mr. Grimm darted after her, his fingertips almost touching her flowing locks. Their chase was like snapshots from a camera, each frame played in slow motion. Shoua felt like she was wearing cement shoes as she tried to escape. Her legs felt heavier with each stride. Mr. Grimm, on the other hand, seemed to have electric surges of energy with each lunge. He was just centimeters from grabbing Shoua's hair.

"*Stop!*" bellowed her father, with Xeng and Grandfather standing next to him.

Mr. Grimm and Shoua came to a screeching halt.

"Mr. Grimm, why were you chasing my daughter?" Shoua's father inquired. The three men stood just a few feet from Shoua and Mr. Grimm.

"Like you even have to ask!" Mr. Grimm answered

after catching his breath. "Your daughter ran away and ruined my perfectly planned trip. She is just as crazy as your father."

"My father and daughter are not crazy."

"Your father thinks there are talking five-toed demon-tigers!" Mr. Grimm sputtered as he gasped for air. "Now your daughter thinks there are dragons!"

As a gust of wind blew through the group, Mr. Grimm touched the bald spot at the top of his head, realizing for the first time his toupee had fallen off in the chase.

"If Mrs. Grimm finds out I lost the children on this camping trip, she will never forgive me," Mr. Grimm confessed. "She is sensitive when it comes to the children."

"Mr. Grimm, our family is grateful for everything you have done for us," Shoua's grandfather said. "But you have to stop treating our Hmong culture as though it is a disease to get rid of."

"But it *is* a disease," said Xeng. "I want people to stop teasing me about my accent, my clothes— my being Hmong."

Xeng's words were like acid to his father and grandfather's ears, stinging and burning at the same time. Their faces were distorted in pain. It hurt them to hear that Xeng was teased and, as a result, didn't have pride in his heritage. However, there was compassion in Shoua's eyes as she looked at her older brother.

"Xeng, there are always going to be things people don't like about you, but you have to learn to like yourself," Shoua said confidently, staring knowingly at Zong. Her younger brother smiled.

"Mr. Grimm, we love this country," her grandfather said. "We love people like you who helped us when we came here with nothing but the flip-flops on our feet and clothes on our backs. However, this country is big, big in its size and big in its ideas—big enough to hold both Little Red Riding Hood and a five-toed tiger."

Mr. Grimm's hawk-eyes opened so wide they looked like saucers. For the first time since Shoua had met him, Mr. Grimm didn't look like he was about to swoop down and snatch prey with his claws.

"I'm sorry," he said. "I was trying to help the only way I knew. I thought I was doing the right thing." Then turning to Xeng, Mr. Grimm sighed before saying, "I never meant for you to think being Hmong was bad. It's not—"

Shoua didn't give Mr. Grimm time to finish his words. Grabbing Zong's hand, she bolted like lightning away from the group toward the dragon. As she got closer, she heard Nanee snort in pain. Mr. Grimm, Xeng, and Shoua's grandfather and father chased after the children, but they had trouble keeping up. Shoua felt as if the winds were carrying her. Her feet didn't touch the ground, and Zong felt like a kite tied to her hands. In no time, the two of them reached the charred hole and slid down to the bottom.

"Nanee, I'm back!" Shoua whispered, crouching over Nanee.

Shoua's family members and Mr. Grimm reached the edge of the crater. Mr. Grimm took in a long breath when he saw the dragon. If he'd had a weaker bladder, he might have wet himself. Shoua's father and Xeng were just as surprised, their eyes bulging out of their sockets. She scanned their pale faces. Only her grandfather looked calm. Shoua watched in amazement as her grandfather slid down the crater with the energy of a child and walked slowly toward the mythical

beast. "Zong," he said, "you found the dragon!"

Her grandfather's face beamed with pride. "Grandson, my shaman spirits said my grandchild had found the dragon. You are the chosen one to help heal the fallen dragon."

Shoua rose, uncurling her spine to stand

tall and face her grandfather. At first she only squeaked like a mouse, then her lips quivered, and her chest heaved as if her broken heart would burst out of her. Shoua fought to control the emotions bubbling inside her, but they had to be released. She began to sob, tears tumbling down her cheeks, mucus dripping from her nose to her mouth. Finally, Shoua's moans became elephant trumpets. The men gazed at her in disbelief.

The volcano of dormant courage, brilliance, and magic erupted from Shoua with the words "*I'm* the chosen one!"

Her words blasted into the late afternoon air, fluttering and drifting in the wind.

"Grandfather, *I* found the dragon!" Shoua said passionately. "You see the world through a veil that makes girls seem useless and boys seem like heroes. You are so blinded by your veil that you couldn't hear your shaman spirits tell you that

I had found the dragon. I AM THE CHOSEN ONE!"

Shoua's words were powerful, stinging her grandfather like a million bees, for those words caused the collapse of everything he ever believed about girls and boys, women and men, and their roles in the world.

The young girl kneeled next to Nanee, pulling a small green feather from her pocket and rubbing it on Nanee's wound. The dragon's belly closed up and white light radiated from the oozing wound until it was completely healed. Shoua's face glowed with the light, as if she was absorbing the dragon's healing powers. For the first time since her birth, Shoua was proud to be a girl.

"I'm sorry, Granddaughter, for doubting you," her grandfather said. "I will never, ever..."

He stopped talking after gazing into Shoua's

determined eyes. He knew she no longer needed him to say it.

Nanee stirred. Now that her magic had been restored, the dragon reared herself up on her powerful hind legs, causing Shoua to let out a "WOW!"

Nanee's pale coloring disappeared, and her scales shined with iridescent colors in the late afternoon sun. Two dragons appeared from mushroom-shaped clouds in the sky and circled the group, flying lower with each circle before landing in front of the hole. They were each the size of semi trucks, and they crushed the trees and bushes as they landed.

"Shoua, thank you," hissed the father dragon. The creature spoke in an ancient language that only Shoua and her grandfather understood. "You have saved our daughter and grandfather."

The young girl took the second loon feather

out of her pocket and it floated toward the dragons until it stuck to one of the dragon father's scales.

"Nanee's grandfather needs the feather, so we must go," hissed the mother dragon. "We have been looking everywhere for Nanee, but couldn't locate her until she got strong again, until her magic returned. Then we sensed her presence."

"I'm sorry for disobeying you," Nanee said.

"We are glad you are safe," answered her mother. "You have shown us that we can trust humans. They can be our friends."

Shoua cleared her throat as though she was going to make a grand speech. Instead she simply said, "Being born a girl, I felt like a bird with its wings clipped. The spirits told me finding the fire ball will give me the wings to fly, and now I understand their words. I want to fly."

~

CHAPTER 8:

Dragons at the Waterfall

~

The wind blew through Shoua's hair causing it to whip fiercely. Riding on top of the soft curve of Nanee's neck, she soared through cotton candy clouds. Underneath her were specks of green dots that were treetops and blue lines in the earth that were streams, and occasionally she saw tiny cars zipping on back roads. She glanced to her right, seeing her grandfather and Mr. Grimm riding on the mother dragon. Mr. Grimm winked and gave her a big thumbs-up. Shoua looked to her left and saw her father and two brothers riding on the father dragon. All three of them had expressions of pure bliss. She giggled with happiness. Her heart fluttered like butterfly wings.

"Where are we going?" she asked Nanee.

"Flying to our secret portal at the waterfall so

we can enter our magic world," Nanee answered.

The dragons flew until they were over a river. They followed the river until it emptied into a waterfall. As the dragons hovered over the waterfall, Shoua noticed the river actually split in two, flowing around a mass of rocks and into two separate waterfalls. The dragons landed at the top of rocks next to the river before it separated and let Shoua and her family off. Misty water from the falls sprayed them as the sound of tumbling water filled their eardrums.

"Shoua will be a powerful shaman one day," hissed the dragon father. "She was born with powerful magic. So take good care of her."

"Nanee will be a powerful dragon," replied Shoua's grandfather. "Take care of her also."

The dragon father and old man stared at each other as if they were making a pact.

Even though they lived in different worlds,

Shoua and Nanee understood they were intertwined and linked for life.

Next, the dragons soared into the sky like rockets and then plunged into the bottom of the waterfall as if the water had sucked them in. A tidal wave of water sprayed the group so there was not a single part of them that was dry. Red rays radiated from the water, and it churned and swirled until the light disappeared.

It was Mr. Grimm who broke the silence by hollering, "Mrs. Grimm is not going to believe this! *Any* of this!"

"The dragon's secret portal is the Devil's Kettle at Judge Magney State Park," said Zong. "I've read about the sink hole at the bottom of the waterfall in books. Scientists have thrown objects to find out where the sink hole leads to, but these objects have disappeared for good. Now we know where they go."

"Great! How will we get back to Ely?" whined Xeng.

"Stop being so negative all the time," Mr. Grimm told the boy. "I can't *wait* to see a talking tiger!"

Shoua smiled. Her grandfather smiled. Everyone smiled.

~

About the Author

Ka Vang is a fiction writer, playwright, poet, and former journalist who has devoted much of her professional life to capturing Hmong folktales on paper. She was born on a CIA military base in Long Cheng, Laos, at the end of the Vietnam War, and immigrated to America in 1980. Her short stories and essays have been featured in six anthologies, including *Riding Shotgun: Women Write about Their Mothers,* published by Borealis Books; *Haunted Hearths and Sapphic Shades: Lesbian Ghost Stories,* published by Lethe Press and a national best-seller in the United Kingdom; and the ground-breaking Asian American anthology *Charlie Chan Is Dead 2: At Home in the World,* published by Penguin Books. In 2009, Ka Vang was featured in the book *Hmong History Makers,* published by Houghton Mifflin, for her work collecting and preserving Hmong folklore from Hmong people across the globe, from Australia to Germany. Her work is used in classrooms and has appeared nationally in magazines and newspapers.

Vang graduated from the University of Minnesota–Twin Cities in 1997 with a bachelor's degree in political science. After additional study in literature at Xavier University in New Orleans and King's College in London, Vang graduated from Minnesota State University–Mankato with a master's in education.

Vang was one of the first Hmong American news reporters in the world, and for ten years was a regular columnist for the *Minnesota Women's Press.* She has received recognition and numerous grants and awards for her writing and leadership, including the Bush Artist Fellowship.

She lives in the Twin Cities in Minnesota with her husband and children.

PHOTO BY PETER YANG

About the Illustrator

Specializing in children's illustration and editorial artwork, Aimee Hagerty Johnson uses acrylic paint, watercolor, graphite, collage, and digital tools to create her whimsical and unique illustrations for kids and adults. A member of the Society of Children's Book Authors and Illustrators, Ms. Johnson earned a BFA in illustration from the Minneapolis College of Art and Design. Her vibrant, energetic illustrations for children and grown-ups can be seen in publications worldwide and at www.aimeehagertyjohnson.com.

COUNCIL ON ASIAN PACIFIC MINNESOTANS

 Minnesota Humanities Center

 CLEAN WATER LAND & LEGACY AMENDMENT

This work is funded with money from the Arts and Cultural Heritage Fund that was created with the vote of the people of Minnesota on November 4, 2008.